T0096327

Worzel goes for a walk!

Will you come too?

Written by Catherine Pickles
Illustrated by Chantal Bourgonje

Kids Hubble & Hattie

I hope you like my Mum's book. She wrote it so that children and dogs can have a great time together throughout their lives. This is the second book in a series that will show you everything dogs and children can do together, happily and safely.

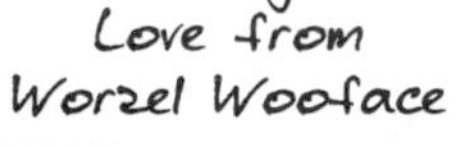

PS If you do know any grownups who like dogs, tell them about the books I wrote!

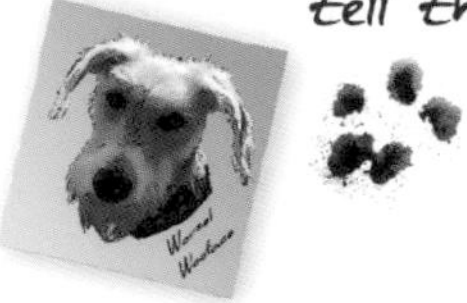

The Hubble & Hattie imprint was launched in 2009, and is named in memory of two very special Westie sisters owned by Veloce's proprietors. Since the first book, many more have been added, all with the same objective: to be of real benefit to the species they cover; at the same time promoting compassion, understanding and respect between all animals (including human ones!)

In 2017, the first Hubble & Hattie Kids! book – *Worzel says hello. Will you be my friend?* – was published, and is now joined by this, the second book in the series.

Other books from our Hubble & Hattie Kids! imprint

9781787111608

9781787113077

978178713060

www.hubbleandhattie.com

First published September 2018 by Veloce Publishing Limited, Veloce House, Parkway Farm Business Park, Middle Farm Way, Poundbury, Dorchester, Dorset, DT1 3AR, England. Tel 01305 260068/Fax 01305 250479/email info@hubbleandhattie.com/web www.hubbleandhattie.com ISBN: 978-1-787112-92-6 UPC: 6-36847-01292-2 British Library Cataloguing in Publication Data – A catalogue record for this book is available from the British Library. Typesetting, design and page make-up all by Veloce Publishing Ltd on Apple Mac. Printed in India by Parksons Graphics.

Foreword

Another delightful book by Catherine Pickles and Chantal Bourgonje. If a picture is worth a thousand words, then lots of pictures are worth millions of words in terms of enhancing the story, which of course, apart from being a more effective means of conveying essential information in fewer pages, saves trees and reduces reading time. The illustrations are spectacular — beyond cute and accurately depicting dog body language.

The message in *Worzel goes for a walk* is simple yet extremely important — teaching children how to have a rich, fun-loving and responsible relationship with their family dogs and how to 'read' dogs that they may meet in other people's homes, in parks, or on walks. It is vital for self-esteem that dog training is successful for children, hence the reward-based training techniques — using brain instead of brawn.

But dogs have feelings too. They can sometimes be aloof, shy, standoffish, wary, fearful, tired, grumpy, rambunctious and rumbustious. Worzel teaches children empathy and respect for dogs, and provides them with the skills and knowledge they need to become the next generation of successful dog trainers and the very best companions.

As entertaining as it is educational, Worzel goes for a walk is a good read. Indeed, parents will enjoy Worzel as much as their children.

Ian Dunbar PhD, BVetMed, MRCVS
Founder of the Association of Professional Dog Trainers

Introduction

Our local beach at Southwold has long been a favourite place for Worzel and I to walk, but recently, like many public spaces in the UK, the rights of dogs to run and play freely have been challenged.

Dogs need spaces where they can exercise but, at the same time, it's up to their owners and guardians to look after these spaces carefully. If we don't, we will lose them.

Worzel goes for a walk has been inspired by the amazing work of Southwold and Reydon Dog Owners group which, through education and campaigning, saved Southwold Beach for dogs.

Now it's time for the next generation of dog lovers to learn the important ways they should look after their dog when they are out for a walk, and also look out for other dogs and people who might not be as confident or able to play.

And, yes – it has to be said – every dog owner needs to pick up their dog's poo: whilst this isn't a job for small people, we should lead by example to ensure that they understand it's absolutely essential and key to dogs continuing to have access to public spaces.

Catherine

All interactions between children and dogs should be supervised by an adult.

Parental Advice

Family trips to the beach; the ubiquitous sun, sea and sand. Time for mum and dad to kick back. Room for the kids and dogs to run around in the fresh air, swimming, splashing, with squeals of excitement. Digging holes, building castles, sandy picnics and the smell of barbeques: it's all exciting sensory stimulation but we have to share the space and be careful not to impact on other people's relaxation time.

Just like people, some dogs may be scared or anxious, injured or ill, or simply having a grumpy day for whatever reason. Even normally friendly dogs may be overwhelmed by all the unusual activity, scents, sights, and sounds.

Worzel goes for a walk can only help young people and their families understand their responsibilities, and this beautiful book is essential reading for everyone who loves dogs.

Charlotte Pither

Charlotte is chair of Southwold and Reydon Dog Owners Group. Part of the group's focus is to improve relationships between non dog- and dog-owning families by encouraging respectful and responsible ownership.

It's a beautiful day to go for a walk
It's my favourite thing to do!

It might be cold but we're off to the beach. Do you want to come along too?

I'll need my lead,
lots of treats
and some bags

In summer the beach is busy and full
With people enjoying the sun

But in winter the beach is peaceful and quiet.

Just seagulls and dogs having fun

We can
paddle

and dance

and splash in
the sea

Jump over the waves and race on the sand

But when I am wet, I wiggle and shake

so you might
want to watch
where you stand

Some of the dogs at the beach are my friends

They're happy
to see me, they
want to play

But others are older,

or worried, or scared

They'd much rather I
played further away

If a dog on a lead comes
towards us
keep me close until he's
gone by

It's not fair to let me
rush up ...

... to dogs who are tired,
or frightened or shy

When I do a poo, it must be picked up

A job no-one likes but it has to be done

Then bag it and bin it, or just take it home

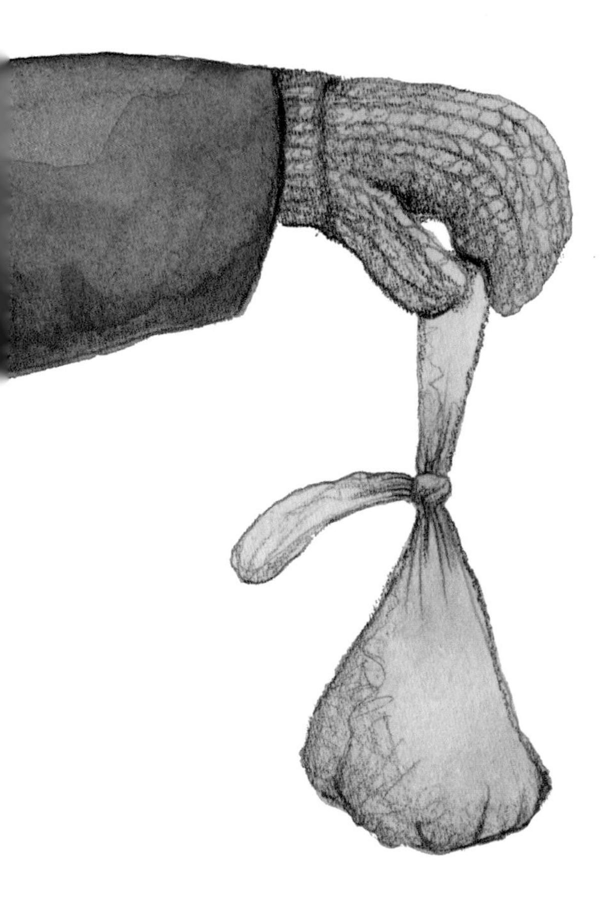

Let's keep the beach clean for everyone

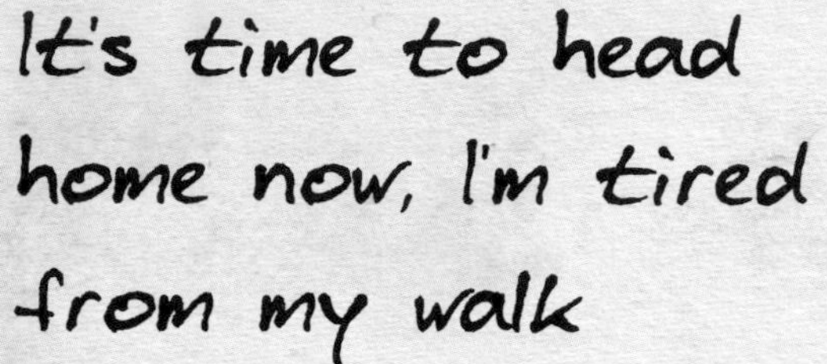

It's time to head
home now, I'm tired
from my walk

Please clip on my lead
now we're ready to go

I'm covered in sand from our games on the beach

And not everyone wants me to say hello!

I'm glad to be home to get warm, clean and dry

A rub with a towel, brush the sand from my feet

I'll rest by the fire to plan our next trip

The games we can play and the friends we will meet

Catherine and Worzel

Catherine Pickles is a teacher, parent, journalist and Worzel's mum. She has owned dogs all her life and regularly fosters lurchers and sighthounds. Author of an hilarious series of books for adults about Worzel, this is Catherine's and Chantal's second children's book about Worzel: the first being *Worzel says hello! Will you be my friend?*

Worzel

Initially a foster dog, from the second Worzel skidded through the door, Catherine knew that he would be her first 'failed foster' – and Worzel Wooface was adopted permanently.

Worzel has always loved running on the beach and, as his home has only a small garden, he loves the wide open spaces where he can stretch his very long legs!

Worzel blogs and writes a regular column for his local newspaper. He is a champion for rescue dogs, and considers himself a Rescue Ambassador, promoting the joys and challenges of second-hand dogs.

In 2016, Worzel won a Heroes of Dog Fest award.

Chantal

Chantal Bourgonje is a Dutch illustrator and writer of picture books, working from her studio in the Wiltshire countryside, where she lives with her partner and two Whippets.

Chantal's inspiration comes from nature, the countryside, and all the living creatures in it.

In 2011, she graduated with a 1:1 Honours degree in Illustration.
Her graduation project was highly commended in the MacMillan Prize, and, in 2013, she was highly commended in the AOI Awards. Since graduating, Chantal has written and illustrated children's picture books, one of which, *Fierce Grey Mouse,* was awarded a Kirkus Star for books of remarkable merit.

Other books illustrated by Chantal are *Worzel says hello!* and *The Lucky, Lucky Leaf*, the first in the Horace & Nim series.